Do you know where Wonderland is? It's the place you visit in your dreams—that strange and wondrous land where nothing is as it seems. Alice learned all about Wonderland one warm, golden afternoon when she fell asleep under a cool, shady tree.

The first strange thing that Alice saw in Wonderland was a white rabbit wearing pants and a waistcoat! He rushed down the path, glancing hurriedly at his watch. "I'm late. I'm late for a very important date. No time to say hello, goodbye. I'm late, I'm late, I'm late, I'm late!"

Alice watched him scurry across a brook and disappear into a hollow tree. "Now, this is curious. What could a rabbit possibly be late for? It must be a party or something."

Alice crossed the brook and peered into the
hollow tree. "What a peculiar place to have a party!"
She squeezed through the opening and found herself
crawling down a dark tunnel. "I really shouldn't do
this. After all, I haven't been invited. And curiosity
often leads to trouble..." The tunnel floor abruptly
ended, and Alice fell down a large hole!

But it wasn't a dirty, musty hole. It was like a tall, thin house. There were bookshelves and cupboards and pictures on the wall. And Alice was falling very slowly, so she had time to look around and think. "Hmm. What if I should fall right through the center of the earth and come out the other side?"

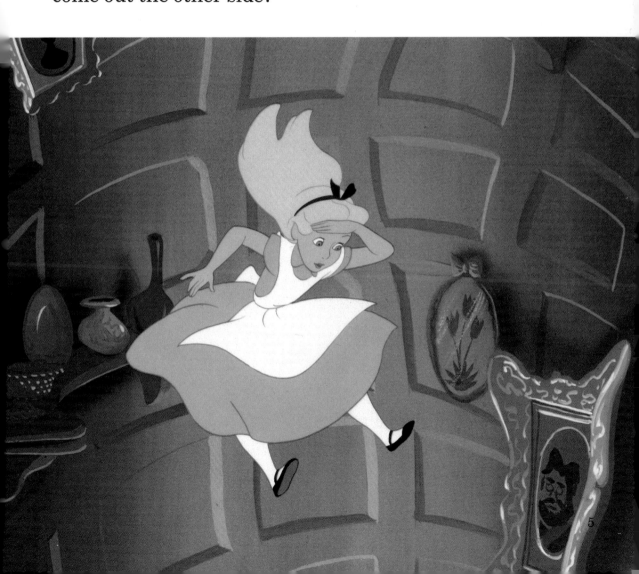

Alice landed with a bump, just in time to see the
White Rabbit disappear through a tiny door. "Oh,
Mister Rabbit. Wait, please!" Alice squeezed through
the door and found herself outside again.

"Oh, dear, I'm sure the White Rabbit came this way."
But when Alice looked around, she found everything
either upside-down or backwards. "Curiouser and
curiouser," thought Alice.

Stranger still, whenever Alice would eat a bit of cake
or take a sip to drink, she would change sizes! Once,
a bite of mushroom sent her shooting up in height.
Her head cleared the treetops and frightened the birds
nesting there.

8

Another bite made Alice shrink so small that the flowers and the rocking-horse-fly towered above her.

Alice also met talking animals in Wonderland. There
was the Walrus and the Dodo and the Caterpillar. They
tried to help Alice with her search for the White Rabbit,

but they mainly took up her time with funny songs and silly races. "Forward, backward, inward, outward, bottom to the top! Makes no difference where you run as long as you don't stop!"

So Alice went off to find the White Rabbit by herself.

Alice came to a clearing, and there stood a small house with pink shutters and a round door. "Now I wonder who lives here?" thought Alice.

Just then, the front door flew open, and out raced the White Rabbit! "Oh me, oh my. I'm awfully late! My fuzzy ears and whiskers took me too much time to shave!"

The White Rabbit looked up to see Alice at the garden gate. "Why, Mary Ann! What are you doing here? Well, don't just do something, stand there! No, no, no—go get my gloves! I'm late!"

"But late for what?" asked Alice.

"My gloves!" said the White Rabbit firmly. So Alice dutifully went to look for them, though she knew full well that she wasn't Mary Ann!

When Alice came back, the White Rabbit was just disappearing through the woods again. "You see, I'm overdue—I'm in a rabbit stew! Can't even say goodbye, hello. I'm late, I'm late, I'm late!"

Alice rushed off into the woods again, only this
time, she was greeted by a funny pair of twins named
Tweedledum and Tweedledee. "Say, 'How do you do'
and shake hands. State your name and business!"
When Alice said her business was finding the White
Rabbit, the two sillies directed her to the Mad Hatter's
tea party.

"Sit down and join us, my dear," said the Mad Hatter.
"Since it's not our birthdays today, the March Hare
and I decided to celebrate our *un*birthdays!"

"Why, then it's my unbirthday today, too!" exclaimed
Alice. And they all celebrated with tea and cake.

THE UNBIRTHDAY SONG

A very merry unbirthday to you, to you.
A very merry unbirthday to you, to you.
It's great to drink to someone, and I
  guess that you will do.
A very merry unbirthday to you!

Statistics prove, prove that you've
  one birthday, one birthday every year.
But there are 364 unbirthdays—
That is why we're gathered
  here to cheer.

A very merry unbirthday to us,
  to us.
A very merry unbirthday to us,
  to us.
If there are no objections, let it be
  unanimous.
A very merry unbirthday to us!

A very merry unbirthday to me. To who?
A very merry unbirthday to me. To you?
Let's all congratulate me with a present, I agree.
A very merry unbirthday to me!

Statistics prove, prove that you've one birthday,
  one birthday every year.
But there are 364 unbirthdays,
Precisely why we're gathered here to cheer.

A very merry unbirthday to all, to all.
A very merry unbirthday to all, to all.
Let's have a celebration, hire a band and rent a hall.
A very merry unbirthday, a very merry unbirthday,
A very merry unbirthday to all!

Alice left the party and next came to a lovely garden where playing cards were working as gardeners. They were all busy painting the roses red. "Why must you do that?" Alice asked the three-of-clubs.

"We planted white roses by mistake, and the Queen will have our heads unless we change them all to red!"

A trumpet blew, and the cards all scampered into line. "Make way for the Queen of Hearts!" called a familiar voice.

Alice peeked around a card to see the White Rabbit leading the royal procession. "So this is why he was hurrying so!" Then Alice spotted the ill-tempered Queen and her timid little husband. Behind them followed a file of stern-looking playing cards.

"Who is this?" snapped the Queen, pointing to
Alice. "Why, it's a little girl. Do you play croquet?"

Alice curtsied. "Yes, Your Majesty. But I really
mustn't stay. I'm trying to find my way home."

"*Your* way?" bellowed the Queen. "All ways here are
my ways. Off with her head!" The Queen's cards rushed
at Alice to carry out their orders!

"Oh, pooh. I'm not afraid of you! Why, you're nothing but a pack of cards." Alice gave the cards a push, and they went flying in all directions.

This made the Queen very angry. "Off with her head!" she roared, and the cards regrouped for another charge!

Suddenly, Alice woke up and found herself still under the shady tree. "Why, it was all a dream. Thank goodness. I've had quite enough of Wonderland for now."

I'M LATE

I'm late, I'm late for a very important date.
No time to say hello, goodbye. I'm late,
    I'm late, I'm late, I'm late.
And when I wave, I lose the time I save.
My fuzzy ears and whiskers took me too much time to shave.

I run, and then I hop, hop, hop. I wish that I could fly.
There's danger if I dare to stop, and here's the reason why—
You see, I'm overdue. I'm in a rabbit stew.
Can't even say goodbye, hello. I'm late, I'm late, I'm late!

Good morning, Mr. Chatterbox. I'd love to stop and chatter,
But in six and seven-eighths minutes, I must meet with
    the Mad Hatter.
The mad, mad, mad, Mad Hatter.
We must chat about a very important matter.

I'm off to see the Queen of Hearts, who lives up in the palace.
And the very moment I'm through with her,
    I've got a date with Alice.
I can't be late for Alice or the Queen of Hearts, who
    lives up in the palace.

I'm late, I'm late for a very important date.
No time to say hello, goodbye. I'm late,
    I'm late, I'm late, I'm late.
And when I wave, I lose the time I save.
My fuzzy ears and whiskers took me too much time to shave.

I run, and then I hop, hop, hop. I wish that I could fly.
There's danger if I dare to stop, and here's the reason why—
You see, I'm overdue. I'm in a rabbit stew.
Can't even say goodbye, hello. I'm late, I'm late, I'm late,
    I'm late, can't wait, I'm late for a very important date,
I'm late, I'm late, I'm late, can't wait, I'm late
    for a very important date. I'm late!

24